I Love You More Than You'll Ever Know

LESLIE ODOM, JR. & NICOLETTE ROBINSON

Illustrated by **Joy Hwang Ruiz**

FEIWEL AND FRIENDS · NEW YORK

$\mathcal{D}$o you remember
when we first met?
It was a moment
I won't soon forget.

Your sparkling aura. Your crooked grin!

Do you remember, my trusted friend?

When I count all my blessings,

you're always number one.

Sweetest of all is ...

we've only just begun.

I love you more than you'll ever know.

You take my hand and then

OFF WE GO!

Day by day,
as I watch you grow,

I love you more than
you'll ever know . . .

I love you so.

So many questions!
You wonder why.

You see the world through watchful eyes.

You're so decisive.
Like it or not.

You make me laugh real hard.
You do that a lot!

Have I told you how much I enjoy your company?

Even on days we're at odds and don't agree.

Hasn't always been easy, but you've always made it fun.

From the day that we met

and with each trip around the sun.

I love you more than
you'll ever know.

You take my hand and then
OFF WE GO!

Day by day,
as I watch you grow—

I love you more than
you'll ever know . . .

I love

you so.

For Lucille and Able:
You were the song before there ever was a song.
—L.O.J. & N.R.

For Aurelia & Agatha, and for all families.
—J.H.R.

A Feiwel and Friends Book • An imprint of Macmillan Publishing Group, LLC • 120 Broadway, New York, NY 10271 • mackids.com • Copyright © 2023 by Lenny and Lucille, Inc. All rights reserved. • Our books may be purchased in bulk for promotional, educational, or business use. Please contact your local bookseller or the Macmillan Corporate and Premium Sales Department at (800) 221-7945 ext. 5442 or by email at MacmillanSpecialMarkets@macmillan.com. • Library of Congress Cataloging-in-Publication Data is available. • First edition, 2023 • The illustrations for this book were created digitally with Procreate. It was designed by Aram Kim. Production was supervised by Kim Waymer, and the production editor was Kat Kopit. Edited by Kat Brzozowski. • Feiwel and Friends logo designed by Filomena Tuosto • Printed in China by RR Donnelley Asia Printing Solutions Ltd., Dongguan City, Guangdong Province • ISBN 978-1-250-26564-7 • 10 9 8 7 6 5 4 3 2 1